FLAMES of M

by Sam George

www.rourkeeducationalmedia.com

Edited by: Keli Sipperley
Cover layout by: Rhea Magaro
Interior layout by: Jen Thomas
Cover Illustration by: Ludovic Salle

Library of Congress PCN Data

Flames of Freedom / Sam George
 (History Files)
 ISBN (hard cover)(alk. paper) 978-1-68191-679-8
 ISBN (soft cover) 978-1-68191-780-1
 ISBN (e-Book) 978-1-68191-880-8
 Library of Congress Control Number: 2016932556

Printed in the United States of America,
North Mankato, Minnesota

Dear Parents and Teachers,

The History Files series takes readers into significant eras in United States history, allowing them to walk in the shoes of characters living in the periods they've learned about in the classroom. From the journey to a new beginning on the Mayflower, to the strife of the Vietnam War and beyond, each title in this series delves into the experiences of diverse characters struggling with the conflicts of their time.

Each book includes a comprehensive summary of the era, along with background information on the real people that the fictional characters mention or encounter in the novel. Additional websites to visit and an interview with the author are also included.

In addition, each title is supplemented with online teacher/parent notes with ideas for incorporating the book into a lesson plan. These notes include subject matter, background information, inspiration for maker space activities, comprehension questions, and additional online resources. Notes are available at: www.RourkeEducationalMedia.com.

We hope you enjoy the History Files books as much as we do.

Happy reading,
Rourke Educational Media

TABLE OF CONTENTS

CHAPTER ONE

———◦———————————◦———

July 18, 1776

On the day the Declaration of Independence was read in Boston, the air was hot and humid.

Jonathan Stone loosened his collar, making room against his skin for whatever breeze might stir and cool him off. He was harvesting wild strawberries in the garden behind the small house he shared with his mother. The strawberry plants were his pride and joy, and if he waited any longer to pick the tender red fruit, he risked losing them entirely.

The days were hot and although he watered the plants every day, still their leaves drooped a little. The stems and leaves were as important for teas as the berries so he worked quickly and efficiently.

A year ago, when his father had been killed

at the Battles of Lexington and Concord, it had been his idea to sell their bit of farm and move to Boston to set up a small shop selling tea and homespun clothing.

Ever since the Townshend Acts, which had ended six years earlier in 1770, colonists had become clever about tea, either smuggling it in from the Dutch or simply making it themselves. Homemade and illegal tea did not taste as good as the tea sold by the East India Company, but to buy and sell tea from the East India Company meant accepting British taxation without representation.

Jonathan still found himself chanting, "No taxation without representation," the singsong slogan that had once been so popular, and that put into words some of the colonists' anger about their mistreatment under British rule.

And then there had been the Boston Tea Party, just three years ago in 1773, when the Sons of Liberty dressed up like Mohawk Indians, climbed aboard East Indian Company boats in the harbor and threw all the tea overboard. The water in the harbor had been stained for days. The Sons of Liberty had gone out in dinghies to push down any boxes of tea that floated up.

But what about tea? Colonists needed their tea.

When they couldn't smuggle it in, they improvised. And Jonathan had become pretty good at improvising, instinctively understanding the art of crafting tea.

So he and his mother set up shop in Boston, hoping for business, which they found, but Jonathan also hoped his mother would find comfort in the security of living in the city. He thought maybe this hope had been realized, but he couldn't be sure. Since his father's death, she had closed up, like a paper fan.

And for himself, he had hoped that by moving to Boston he would be closer to the heart of the revolution. He longed to be a part of the freedom movement his father had helped start, even though he did not speak of that longing with his mother. He didn't know how she would react. All of her family was back in England. Her response to the war had been less clear than her husband's.

That she worried about her son, though, was obvious.

"You have many fine ideas," she told him, when she found out he had been to a Sons of Liberty meeting with Simeon. "You're like your father, always looking to the future." She smiled sadly. "But some of your ideas contradict my own."

"Like what?" he said.

"Like about your safety," she said. "You think nothing bad can happen to you because you're just a boy. But you need to be careful. Please, be careful."

He hadn't liked being told he was "just a boy," but neither did he want to cause her further heartache and worry.

So, for the most part, he stayed close to home, working in the garden, working in the shop, testing new varieties of herbs and trying out different combinations of flavors.

Adding dried strawberries to tea was one of his fine ideas, one his mother approved of. Over the course of a year, their tea had earned a fine reputation in the neighborhood and had won them a number of devoted customers, even a few British sympathizers. His mother served them—Jonathan couldn't bear to.

Still another of his ideas had been to set up a table and chairs near the window so that customers might take tea, and sit and talk.

This worked out well because Jonathan had a need for information. When people talked, he listened.

And sometimes they left behind pamphlets circulated by the Sons of Liberty.

One time, Mr. and Mrs. Prickford sat at the table, taking a break from the harsh winter snow.

Mrs. Prickford said, "This snow is dreadful, isn't it?"

"Dreadful, yes," said Mr. Prickford.

"I daresay we have weeks of it left."

"I daresay you're right. I see no sign of spring in all this snow."

"No sign at all, I'm afraid."

Mrs. Prickford sighed and went on to discuss the dreadful condition of the drapes in their dining room. Their conversation did not hold Jonathan's interest, but when they departed, they left behind on the table a pamphlet called *Common Sense*, by Thomas Paine.

In the pamphlet, Jonathan read, "In America the law is king. For as in absolute governments the king is law, so in free countries the law ought to be king; and there ought to be no other."

Jonathan didn't fully understand Thomas Paine's pamphlet, but he did get the feeling that beyond the fighting, the war was about ideas; ideas about what role a government should play in people's lives.

And what of the fighting?

Where was General Washington? What was the Continental Congress saying about the war effort? What was the plan? Was there a plan? Did anyone have a plan?

Sometimes, from his perspective, the war effort seemed disorganized and random. He hoped he was wrong. He hoped he only thought this because he knew so little.

He listened to conversations on the street. He heard news passed about, sometimes in whispers, sometimes loudly proclaimed.

What he did know was that the British underestimated the zeal with which the colonists fought.

He knew George Washington's forces were growing stronger, and that when the Continental Congress met, their words grew bolder, their dreams bigger. But how exactly, he couldn't say.

And while the war raged, mostly beyond the city limits, he crafted tea.

He was proud of his tea, but something else was brewing.

He began to observe he was not alone in listening for news of the war.

His mother tried to hide her interest in the war from him, but he saw it anyway, in the way she watched the street, in the way she listened closely for news of fighting and the whereabouts of General Washington. He heard it in her conversations before she turned quiet when he drew near.

He knew she wanted to protect him, but at fourteen years old and taller than she, it was only a matter of time before he must choose to be safe, or join the revolution and fight for freedom as his father had.

Some people in Boston spoke of staying neutral as a way to ride out the war without suffering personal loss. He suspected this was his mother's intention, though she never said so outright and he never asked her. She was conflicted, he knew that. When he was conflicted, she gave him space. He would do the same for her.

Although he respected his mother's struggle to identify her loyalties, staying neutral did not seem right to Jonathan. He did not know his grandparents in England. His family was here, in Massachusetts. British soldiers had killed his father. To him, there was no conflict of interest. To him, the British must be fought.

He understood the strong and sometimes desperate desire for safety—would he not give anything to have his father back with them? But his father had believed in freedom more than the importance of his own life.

To believe something is worth living for; worth dying for. That was the lesson his father had taught him, the lesson that remained Jonathan's guide for every day.

"Jonathan?" Mrs. Stone called from in the house.

"In the garden!"

Mrs. Stone stood in the doorway, a basket of bread and vegetables on her arm. She untied her bonnet and touched her pinned-up brown hair. "How are the strawberries?"

"The berries are fine but the leaves look parched." He stood, stretching out his legs, his pants too short. He held the basket forward so that she could inspect the cuttings.

She picked up a limp stem. "Dunk them in chilled water. They should perk right up."

"Yes, Ma'am."

She turned to go back inside but paused in the doorway. "Have you been out yet today?"

Jonathan glanced at the sun. It must have been about noon. "Just to deliver the cloth to Mrs. Winston."

She nodded.

He knew what she wanted to say. She wanted to ask him to not go to the reading this afternoon at the State House.

The whole city was talking about the pamphlet written by Thomas Jefferson, John Adams, Benjamin Franklin, and others. It had been read in Philadelphia on the fourth of July, just fourteen days ago, and now today it was going to be read at the State House.

The pamphlet was called The Declaration of Independence.

Jonathan desperately wanted to be there to hear it read, and should his mother ask him not to, on account of potential violence, he didn't know if he could respect her wishes. History was happening. He wanted to be a part of it. If he didn't mention the reading, maybe she wouldn't ask him to stay home, and then his conscience would be clear.

She turned to go back inside but paused. She struggled to find words for what she wanted to say.

Jonathan waited.

She frowned, pulling down the lines around her mouth. They were lines of sorrow that had showed up the day her husband died and had seemed to deepen, and lengthen, every day after.

"There is a reading today. A pamphlet, from the Continental Congress, from Philadelphia."

"Yes."

"You know about it, of course."

"I've heard about it, yes."

"Not everyone in Boston is a Patriot. Some are still loyal to the king."

"I know." He held his breath.

She nodded. "I worry," she said softly.

"Yes, Mother." He didn't know what to do. His arms hung limply at his side. He knew she worried for him, for his safety alone. He felt so torn.

It had been only five months since Evacuation Day, when General George Washington led the Continental Army to Dorchester Heights with cannons captured at Fort Ticonderoga. In the face of so much cannon force, after an eleven-month siege, the British decided they'd be better off leaving Boston entirely and had fled north to Nova Scotia.

There was probably no man in the thirteen colonies better loved than General Washington. Since the day he had booted the British out of Boston, many Bostonians were eager to fully participate in the war, unfettered now by Redcoat occupation.

However, remaining Loyalists, sometimes called Tories, feared the Redcoat departure signaled King George's declining power in the colonies and wondered whether they should themselves leave, or at the very least take up arms to defend the king, which many did.

Sometimes one's neighbor was the enemy. Sometimes one's family member was the enemy.

And so Boston continued to be roiled in suspicion, on the brink of violence.

Mrs. Stone fingered her bonnet, studying the view of the street from the garden. There was so much she wanted to say but couldn't find words for. "Take care of the strawberries," she finally said, and went inside the house.

"The Declaration of Independence." Jonathan said the words out loud. What impact could a simple document have?

Chapter Two

Jonathan gathered the strawberries and clippings into a basket and brought them into the front room of their small house, which served as their shop. His mother had hung up her bonnet and donned her apron. She organized jars of tea leaves on a shelf. She turned their names outward. She lifted each one and dusted beneath. She rearranged them. Jonathan could tell she was troubled.

"It's a beautiful day," he said cheerfully, hoping to relieve her mind.

"A bit hot, if you ask me," she said, smiling, but the smile was half-hearted and did not reach her eyes. There was a time when she had laughed easily. Not many people these days laughed easily anymore.

Maybe Simeon did, but then Simeon had no family to fear for, and so he embraced the war with enthusiasm, maybe even fecklessness. Still, he was a good friend and Jonathan was always glad to see him.

Jonathan had just set his basket on the thick wooden counter, worn from use, when Simeon himself burst through the door.

Simeon's red hair was consistently wild, but today the whole of him looked wild, from his hair to his bright green eyes, to his hands that flapped around like a pigeon's wings. "They're going to read it today!" he whooped. "You'll come, won't you? You can't miss this. You just can't. Please tell me you'll come."

"Simeon, please," Mrs. Stone said. "There is no need to be so loud. This room is rather small for such volume."

"Oh, good day, Mrs. Stone! Beautiful weather we're having, wouldn't you say?" said Simeon, softening his tone, or at least trying to.

"It's too hot," Mrs. Stone said. She had never fully embraced Jonathan's friendship with Simeon. She said Simeon was mercurial, unpredictable.

"It's a beautiful day for liberty, however hot it is," Simeon said. "They're reading it today! Today! Those Tories, what's left of them, anyway, are really going to hate this. I can't wait to see their faces—Declaration of Independence! Doesn't that sound fine? I think it sounds fine. I think it sounds more than fine." He did a little dance. "Independence!"

Jonathan grinned. His friend had more energy than five people combined. His battle to keep his body calm was visible to all, which was probably why his employer, Colonel Thomas Craft, sent him on so many errands, so that his energy would be put to use running through the streets of the city instead of stifled doing work in the house.

That he worked for Colonel Thomas Craft, one of the Sons of Liberty, and a leader in the city, worked well for Jonathan because it gave him access to inside information about the war and the activities of the Continental Congress.

"Jonathan has much to do, today, Simeon,"

Mrs. Stone said. Her hands shook as she tried to take a cover off a jar. Jonathan reached to help her. "The strawberries are just picked, as you can see."

Simeon glanced at the basket on the counter. "Yes, ma'am," he said, though he looked at Jonathan and widened his eyes. Jonathan knew his meaning. What were strawberries and tea compared to revolution? At this moment, everything revolved around liberty. Liberty from the tyranny of King George.

"What can I get for you today, Simeon?" Mrs. Stone said. "Or did you come just to dance on my clean floor?"

"Mrs. Craft would like a pouch of the black currant, if you have any," Simeon said, clasping his hands in front in an effort to stay still.

"Certainly we have some," Mrs. Stone said. She checked the jars on the shelf. "Perhaps in the back. Give me one moment." She disappeared through the door and Simeon turned his full attention to Jonathan.

"You must come with me," he whispered loudly. "I'll throw a feedsack over your head and kidnap you if I must."

Jonathan shook his head. "It didn't work the last time you tried. Why would it this time?"

"I'll use a larger sack this time around."

"Even so, I'm too fast for you to catch."

Jonathan bounced from foot to foot like a boxer.

Simeon feigned a punch. "You think so, do you?"

Jonathan dodged lightly. "You can run longer, but I can run faster."

"Is that a challenge, then?" Simeon said. "I'll race you, right now, to the State House."

"I can't."

"We are declaring our independence, Jonathan! The war *means* something now. We have a goal, a glorious goal. How does that not move you?"

"My mother," he started to say.

"Tell her to come with us. Or just come now, without telling her. History is happening right now and you're going to take care of your strawberry plants? Really, Jonathan? Where are your priorities? Come on! Come with me now. If she's angry later, it will fade."

In fact, Jonathan's heart was pounding against his ribcage. "The Declaration of Independence" did not sound like a bunch of troublemaking colonists rebelling against their king, as he knew the British saw them, but like an organized people proclaiming their freedom.

Independence.

Self-rule. No more of the king's taxes, no more of the king's edicts, no more being a part of King George's dominion without a voice in government. The colonists would make their own government, beholden to no one. As his father had dreamed of. As he dreamed of. As he suspected his mother dreamed of.

Mrs. Stone returned.

The boys fell silent.

Simeon stared at his shoes.

Jonathan watched his mother. She moved efficiently. Everything she took out was returned to its rightful place. Any small bit of loose tea that spilled, she cleaned up within seconds. Her attention to detail made their business shine.

She must have felt his eyes on her. She stopped suddenly and looked at him.

He stood up straight.

She studied him for a moment, seeming to take in his height, the shadow on his chin, the way he stood with his shoulders back.

"You look like your father," she said. "More and more every day. You sound like him too."

"He was a good man," Jonathan said, feeling his throat close. He blinked, trying to keep tears from falling.

"He was the best man I ever knew."

Simeon, apparently aware of being an outsider in the conversation, now stared at the wall as if trying to give them privacy.

Mrs. Stone turned her attention to Simeon. "I'm glad you have not thrown a feedsack over my son's head."

Simeon blushed.

"The walls are thin in our home, for all your attempts at whispering."

"It was an idle threat, Mrs. Stone. An idle threat only. Just a joke."

"I don't approve of your jokes, Simeon."

"No, ma'am."

"Independence," she muttered.

"It's what has always been spoken of," Jonathan said.

"Just never so officially."

"It's long overdue."

"Yes. It is." She sighed. "Long overdue."

Jonathan hesitated, then said what was on his mind. "I want to hear the words spoken, Mother. It will mean validation—validation for his death. He died for independence."

"Do not tell me for what he died. I know full well." She angrily thrust the pouch of black currant tea at Simeon. "Tea." She glared at him, holding out her hand. "And don't you try tempting my son into trouble. He's made of sturdier stuff than you know."

"Yes ma'am. I mean, no, ma'am. I mean…" Simeon shook his head. Without another word he fumbled through his coins to find the right amount and dropped them into her upturned palm. "Thank you, Mrs. Stone," he muttered. He gave a half wave to Jonathan then scurried to the door and out into the street.

Jonathan longed to follow him, to run freely through the streets as he did. He wondered what it would be like to be responsible for no one, to be free to fight when he believed it right. And yet, he thought, what point is there in fighting at all if you have no one to fight for?

His mother stared out the window, lost in thought.

"I won't go, you know," he said softly. "We will hear about it soon enough. Simeon will remember a fair amount and recite it to us, I reckon. What he misses someone else will know, and all the pieces will shortly be in place. It matters not whether we are there for the actual reading." He said this but he believed otherwise, for there was power in people coming together, in showing unity as a group, in raising their voices simultaneously in anger, or celebration, or fear, or whatever emotions impel them to join together. The coming together mattered.

"It isn't the reading itself," his mother said.

"Then what is it?"

She retied her apron, saying, "It's that we're on the fence and I know we need to get off. I know that I need to get off. I lose sleep over being lukewarm, being uncommitted like this while other people risk their safety, risk their lives." She paused. "While other people lose their lives."

Jonathan waited. He could hardly believe what he was hearing.

"Your father wanted freedom for you more than anything else in the world." She wiped away tears. "But he would not want your freedom bought by anyone. He would have you do your part. And he would have me do mine." She added softly, "I would have me do mine."

She turned from the window and faced Jonathan, her expression determined. "We will go to the reading. We will go together. We will use it as a new beginning for us. Our country will fight for independence, and this is our country. We will fight as well. We will not stand and watch while others do it for us."

Jonathan picked her up and hugged her.

That he could pick her up surprised them both and they laughed.

"Truly," she said, "You are no longer a child." She patted his shoulders and smiled.

"Father would be so proud to hear you," he told her.

She nodded. "I know. I feel him with me sometimes. I think he has been waiting for me to say these words. As you have been waiting, I know."

Jonathan smiled. "What made up your mind?"

"I heard this morning at the market," said his mother, "That John Adams had a hand in writing the document."

"John Adams, cousin of Sam Adams?"

His mother nodded. "More importantly, husband to Abigail Adams, who once paid me a great kindness as a child. I want to hear what he has helped write."

"Then let's go!"

"Not so fast, my boy. We need to take care of these strawberry clippings. Maintaining our young business is one way we can offer practical assistance in the war effort."

"What do you mean?"

"We are a part of the industry of Boston. If everyone shuttered their shops, whose profits would pay for the army? Who would have a little extra to donate to charity?"

"I see your point," Jonathan said. He selected a strawberry from the basket, inspecting it.

"Then let us dry herbs and leaves and fruit to keep our shop open, so that we can do our part."

His mother joined him at the counter as a customer arrived and the bell on the door chimed. "And let us do our work quickly," she added quietly, "So that we might make our way to the State House and find a good place to stand. I want to hear every word."

Chapter Three

But it wasn't until forty-five minutes later that Mrs. Stone announced the shop was in tidy enough condition to leave. The strawberry plants had been hung upside down to dry, the floor swept, the counter cleaned, empty jars cleaned, jars of tea organized, and three more customers had come in for orders.

One of them was Mrs. Wilson from across the street. She was a small thin woman with a permanent scowl. She had lost her son at Lexington and Concord but instead of blaming the British, she blamed the Sons of Liberty for tempting him to fight with the promise of freedom. She claimed he didn't know what he had gotten into until it was too late.

"Independence. Bah!" she said, her chin in the air. "An impossible dream." She always said that, every time she came to buy tea. She always wanted to talk about the war and always declared its pursuit "an impossible dream."

"Will you be going to the State House then, Mrs. Wilson?" Jonathan always tried to be especially kind to her. She was grouchy, sure, but she had no one left. She lived alone with her grief, which Jonathan thought must be like a prison. His own grief he shared with his mother, whose love and care worked like a salve to heal the inflamed parts of his heart. But to be alone, suddenly alone with all the pain of loss, it would be too much.

"No, I'm not going, of course not." Mrs. Wilson waved her hand as if brushing away the suggestion. "Such a lot of talk. And for what? The British army, the British navy, we are no match for them. They will *crush* us. Just you watch."

She shook her finger at Jonathan's mother. "You mind this one here." She indicated Jonathan. "You will lose him soon enough and then you'll be alone like me." She narrowed her eyes at them both.

Then she said, "Good day to you both," and bundled up her tea and stalked out the door, the bell ringing cheerfully to see her go.

"She is deeply unhappy," Jonathan said.

"She has reason to be," Mrs. Stone said. "Put that box there, under the counter, the mop behind the door, and then shall we go? We have a delivery to make."

Jonathan followed her out the door and waited as she locked it. "Can't it wait until after the reading? I fear we are going to miss it." He made no comment regarding Mrs. Wilson's jabs to his mother about being left alone should he go off to soldier and die. Best to let that kind of angry threat roll off.

"It's for Mr. Jansen."

"Oh. I see." As much as he wanted to hurry to the State House immediately, he knew Mr. Jansen needed tea with which to take his medicine and if he didn't take it in a timely fashion, he risked his life. And yet...

"He's a Tory, you know," he said.

"Everyone knows he's a Tory, Jonathan."

Jonathan didn't dare say what he was thinking, but she read his mind. "The whole point of freedom, Jonathan, is to be friends and neighbors with people who think differently than us. If freedom is what we are fighting for, then we are fighting, too, for Mr. Jansen and all his Tory leanings. The hardest part about freedom is accepting and defending people who aren't just like us. And besides, what better way to win him to our side than with timely deliveries and kind words?"

"You think those things really make a difference?"

"I know they do." She held him back as he made to cross the street and a huge carriage rumbled past.

The streets were busy. Most everyone was heading toward the State House with hurried steps and expectant faces.

An elderly man in a smart suit tipped his hat to them. "Mrs. Stone. Jonathan," Judge

Mariner said. "Going to the State House, are you?"

"Yes, sir," Jonathan replied.

Judge Mariner nodded. "Sheriff Greenleaf should be reading within the hour. History will be made today. We will all bear witness." He seemed to want to say more, but Mrs. Stone linked her arm through Jonathan's and set her gaze forward.

Judge Mariner was a perceptive man. He tipped his hat. "Afternoon, ma'am. Jonathan."

"Good afternoon, Judge Mariner," Jonathan said.

The judge crossed the street, dodging between horses, carts, and pedestrians to where his daughter waited for him, arms laden with parcels.

"He's nice," Jonathan said.

"Don't start with me, young man."

Smiling, Jonathan held his tongue.

"Walk faster," Mrs. Stone said. Within minutes they arrived at a tidy yellow house with green trim. "Here we are." They ascended the stairs and knocked on the door.

Nobody answered.

"Mr. Jansen?" Mrs. Stone called. She knocked again.

They heard from within a shuffling and then slowly the latch turned and even more slowly the door opened to a pair of intelligent brown eyes set below shaggy grey eyebrows.

"What do you want?" Mr. Jansen said.

Mrs. Stone was all business. "Mr. Jansen, I have your tea delivery. You are expecting me, as you expect me every week and sometimes twice a week. Please open the door."

Mr. Jansen considered this then swung the door open to a long and elegantly furnished hallway. "Trying to keep me taking my medicine, are you, Mrs. Stone? Trying to ensure I stay alive long enough to see these childish colonies throw off the loving care of their king, are you?"

"King George would have you take your medicine, Mr. Jansen."

"Bah. King George has more important things to think about."

"In any case, here is your tea," Mrs. Stone said. Without waiting for permission, she opened the slim drawer of the hallway desk and extracted a small number of pills from a box. She left them lying there and placed next to them the pouch of tea. "Do take them, on time, as Dr. Williams prescribed."

Mr. Jansen sniffed indignantly. "I always do."

"You do not."

Mr. Jansen shrugged. "When I forget, it is because my books hold me hostage."

"Yes, blame the books, as ever. I would love to stay to see that you take those pills, but my son and I are attending the reading at the State House and are in a hurry to secure ourselves an excellent position to see and hear all."

Mr. Jansen narrowed his eyes. They nearly disappeared beneath his eyebrows.

"The Declaration of Independence." He

spat the words.

Mrs. Stone straightened. "So you've heard."

"Of course I've heard. Who hasn't heard?"

When he looked back on that moment at a later time, Jonathan couldn't say what it was that compelled him to speak, but, surprising himself more than anyone, he said, "Would you care to join us, Mr. Jansen?"

His mother's jaw dropped.

Mr. Jansen's eyes popped wider than they seemed capable of.

"Jonathan," Mrs. Stone said. "I'm sure Mr. Jansen's political proclivities would prevent him from participating in this afternoon's reading."

Mr. Jansen stroked his chin. "Yes, my political proclivities." He stared at Jonathan a moment. "What do you know of King George, child?"

"I'm not a child. I'm fourteen. I know King George does not value the colonies except for the resources and money he is able to extract from them."

"King George is your *king*! He is your sovereign, by the grace of God, and when you rebel against him you rebel against God himself."

"I don't believe God gives one man such power over other men," Jonathan said. "Not even a king."

"And what do you think will happen if the colonies are free? Who will rule you all?"

"We will rule ourselves."

"With what form of a government?"

"What form?" Jonathan repeated. "I—I don't know." He looked to his mother for help. She only raised an eyebrow. "A monarchy of our own?" he stammered. "One that listens to its people?" He suddenly realized the depth of his lack of knowledge. He hadn't thought about what the colonies would actually do with their freedom once won. "I don't know," he admitted. "We'll figure it out. After the war. The Congress will decide, I guess."

"Ah, yes, the Congress. The Congress has many ideas, I am sure. But have they any idea what they will do with themselves after the war? Will the colonies then fight amongst themselves, as they already do?"

"We don't fight with arms."

"Not yet, you don't."

Jonathan was at a loss for words. He hadn't considered the possibility of the colonies continuing to war amongst themselves, and he didn't like not knowing how to respond to Mr. Jansen. He couldn't find the words he needed. He didn't know the answers. He realized how desperately he wanted war with England to be the answer to all the colonies' problems, when in fact, if they won the war, new and different problems would arise, possibly no less complicated than the ones they faced now.

His mother put a hand on his arm. "It's time we leave."

Mr. Jansen had grown red in the face and spittle collected in the corners of his mouth. He suddenly grabbed his cane and hat. "I think I will come with you after all, Mrs.

Stone. With you and your son who wonders what kind of a government he is fighting for."

"Your medicine, Mr. Jansen," Mrs. Stone cautioned.

"Bah! Of what importance is one's health when one's country is at war?" He glared at Jonathan, his eyes flashing.

Jonathan disliked him greatly. He felt threatened by him, by his words, and angry with himself for not knowing how to respond.

The truth was, he hadn't considered before that the colonies were fighting without knowing what the end of the war might look like. What kind of a government would they have? Would there be peace once independence was won? Or would there be continued fighting? It's true the colonies didn't always get along. In fact, they argued rather frequently. They were united at the moment only because England was their common enemy. But would they remain united once, and if, England was defeated?

"Come, Jonathan," Mrs. Stone said.

Mr. Jansen had already left the house and was making an awkward attempt at descending the stairs with the aid of his cane.

Mrs. Stone rushed to help him and Jonathan wondered at her ability to be kind to their enemy.

He followed them down the stairs, feeling bothered and angry and now suddenly wary of where they were heading, now that they had a Tory with them.

Chapter Four

The streets had grown more crowded. Despite their smiles and eager steps, mothers held tightly to the hands of their children. Couples walked with their arms around each other as if worried they might be pulled apart.

Groups of boys Jonathan's age stood on corners appraising people as they passed, calling out greetings to some, and angry words at others.

Jonathan's sense of dread increased.

The boys spotted Mr. Jansen.

"Jansen! Jansen, you Tory!" they shouted. "Only patriots to the State House. Only patriots, Jansen. You are not a patriot, you king-loving traitor!"

Among the group of boys was one Jonathan sometimes went swimming with in the harbor, a boy named Charles May. Charles stepped forward and jutted out his chin, his blue eyes flashing. He held a stick and looked ready to swing it. "Jonathan Stone, are you with that Tory traitor?"

Jonathan glanced at his mother who was firmly gripping Mr. Jansen's arm, guiding him forward. He knew she didn't want Mr. Jansen along with them either, and that his being with them was attracting the kind of anger and violence she had worried about. And yet she didn't leave his side.

Neither would Jonathan leave his mother's side. "Hey Charles, gone swimming lately?" he called. "It's warm enough, that's for sure. How about Wednesday? You free Wednesday?"

Jonathan's friendly tone seemed to put Charles off. He frowned and chewed on his bottom lip. "Yeah, Wednesday's good." He paused before adding, "You be careful out there, Stone. Watch your back now, you hear?"

Jonathan raised his hand in acknowledgment.

Then, ignoring the taunts from the other boys, he hurried to catch up to his mother.

When he reached her she said, "Stay close to me. I don't want to lose you."

He nodded. He knew she meant she didn't want to lose him in the crowd, but he understood the deeper meaning, as well.

They made their way to Devonshire Street and saw ahead of them the State House, a three-story tall brick building with its elaborate steeple, and on the roof, seven-foot-tall statues of a lion and unicorn, symbols of the British monarchy. The first floor of the building housed a Merchant's Exchange, and various government organizations met in the other areas of the building, with the basement being devoted to warehouse space.

It was here, six years ago in front of the building on Devonshire Street, that disgruntled colonists threw snowballs and sticks and stones at British soldiers who in turn opened fire. Several colonists were killed and the event became known as the Boston Massacre.

Jonathan had only been eight years old at the time but he remembered how angry his father had been.

"King George cares nothing for us," his father had said. "Nothing. He cares only for the riches of the land. He cares nothing for the people. Parliament is even worse, taxing us the way they do, and who is over there speaking for us? Nobody. Nobody. We mean nothing to England save for what we produce, for the wealth on which we are taxed." For a man who spoke only out of necessity, even a short tirade such as this was surprising to those around him, including his family.

It was shortly after the Boston Massacre that his father made the decision to fight against England, against the protestations of his wife and the wide-eyed wonderment of his son.

His father told him, "You will understand. One day, Jonathan, you will understand the meaning of injustice and you, too, will raise your voice."

How Jonathan wished his father were with him now. People respected him. They sought his advice. They listened when he spoke. If he were here now, his mother would not feel unsafe.

They were on the fringe of the crowd, standing near the Bunch of Grapes tavern, now overflowing with people holding mugs of ale.

Colonel Crafts' artillery regiment lined the streets. Other military units did too, giving a sense of order but also indicating the potentially inflammatory nature of the speech about to be made.

Jonathan didn't know if seeing all those soldiers standing at attention made him feel safe or more wary.

"We need to get closer," Mrs. Stone said. "No sense standing back here. We won't hear a thing."

Jonathan stood on his tiptoes and spotted an

opening midway through the crowd. "Follow me." He moved in front of his mother and Mr. Jansen, making sure they were holding onto him and to each other, then he began pushing his way through the crowd, meeting a good deal of resistance.

"Watch out, lad!"

"Gads, you fool, where do you think you're going? There's no space up there, you know."

"Pardon me," Jonathan said. "Excuse me. So sorry. You're very kind." They reached about midway through the crowd when Simeon slapped Jonathan's shoulder and said cheerfully, "Jonathan! Mrs. Stone! You came!" His beaming face was a welcome sight.

But as he took in the sight of Mr. Jansen with them, his smile dropped and his eyes grew dark. "This is no place for a Tory."

"You know Mr. Jansen?" Jonathan said.

"I make it my business to know the names of Tories in the neighborhood."

Mr. Jansen snorted. "I came of my own accord, ignorant lad. I came to hear the traitorous speech be made."

Simeon's face turned red. "Traitorous speech?"

Jonathan laid a hand on Simeon's arm. "Peace," he said. "We all have a right to be here."

"Are you with him?" Simeon said, shaking off Jonathan's hand. "You brought him?"

"He came with us."

"He's a king-loving Tory!"

"He has a right to be here. This is still his country, too." Even as he said it, Jonathan wasn't sure if it was true or not. Who had a right to be here, really? Were Tories now traitors, whereas before, Patriots were considered traitors? When did that shift happen? Did it happen when the British left Boston? There didn't seem to be clear guidelines to these kinds of things. There didn't seem to be a list of rules they were to follow. Although, he thought, treating all people with respect seemed like an important rule in times of peace and in times of war, regardless.

"He's a customer," Jonathan continued, wondering if he sounded like he was making an excuse, and if so, if that was cowardice. And why was he feeling so on guard, so defensive, with his friend?

"You should stop doing business with Tories," Simeon said.

Jonathan looked at his mother. Was this true? Were they doing business with the enemy?

"Everyone has a right to drink tea, Simeon, no matter their political affiliations," Mrs. Stone said coldly.

"Hear, hear!" Mr. Jansen interjected.

Simeon spat, narrowly missing Mr. Jansen's shoes. "When you associate with traitors, some might assume you yourself are one."

"But you wouldn't, would you Simeon," Jonathan said.

Simeon hesitated, his fists clenched. He opened his mouth to speak but Jonathan didn't hear his answer, for just then a cheer went up through the crowd as the door to the balcony opened and Sheriff William Greenleaf stepped out, followed by Colonel Crafts.

Mr. Jansen scowled ferociously.

"Independence!" someone shouted.

"Read it out, Sheriff! Read it nice and loud now, I forgot my ear piece!"

"Take your time, Sheriff. I don't want to miss a single word!"

Sheriff Greenleaf raised his hand for silence. He held up a paper. His shaking hands were visible even from where Jonathan stood. The sheriff's mouth moved, but no one could tell if there were words coming out.

"Are there words coming out of that mouth?" someone called.

"What?"

"I can't hear you!"

"Cat got your tongue, Sheriff?"

"How will you win the war if you all cannot even talk?" Mr. Jansen muttered scornfully.

"I'll tell you how," Simeon answered, raising his fists.

"You and your fists," Mr. Jansen said. "You think I am afraid of you, lad? You are but a boy. None of your ideas are your own. When you have ideas of your own, *then I will fear you*."

Jonathan stepped between the old man and his friend.

"Listen, Simeon," he said. "We are here to listen, not to fight. Please."

Sheriff Greenleaf stood there for a few minutes, his voice inaudible, until Colonel Crafts kindly touched him on the shoulder.

They discussed something and then they both nodded and seemed to come to some arrangement.

Greenleaf spoke, reading from the script, and Colonel Crafts acted as his herald, launching the words out into the eager crowd.

His voice filled the square. Perhaps peoples' memories were full of his military heroics, most recently his decisive victory in driving British ships out of Boston Harbor just over a month earlier. The first words he spoke were drowned out by cheering.

He held up his hand and while slow to come, silence soon filled the square.

"When in the course of human events," he called out, *"it becomes necessary for one people to dissolve the political bands which have connected them with another, and to assume among the powers of the earth, the separate and equal station to which the laws of nature and of nature's God entitle them, a decent respect to the opinions of mankind requires that they should declare the causes which impel them to the separation."*

Jonathan shivered at the word, "separation."

The colonel was reading the crowd. He paused for emphasis, possibly moved by his own presentation, his own thunderous voice.

"We hold these truths to be self-evident,

that all men are created equal, that they are endowed by their creator with certain unalienable rights, that among these are life, liberty and the pursuit of happiness."

Jonathan felt a sudden urge to cry.

All men are created equal.

All men are created equal.

All men.

He knew this included his mother standing next to him. He knew this included Mr. Jansen and his opposing political views. It included every man, woman, and child in the crowd.

All. All men are equal.

His father would have been glad to know those words. His father would have repeated them over and over again, as Jonathan did now to himself, quietly, and as he heard others around him doing, whispering the words, implanting them like seeds in their memories, in their hearts.

All men are created equal.

Colonel Crafts continued.

Jonathan hardly dared to breathe. It seemed no one else in the crowd did either. The whispering ceased. No one wanted to miss whatever was to come. They were hungry to hear every word.

"The history of the present King of Great Britain is a history of repeated injuries and usurpations, all having in direct object the establishment of an absolute tyranny over these states. To prove this, let facts be submitted to a candid world."

At this, Mr. Jansen raised his fist and shouted, "Long live King George! Long live King George! Long live King Geo—"

Without even knowing how it happened, Mr. Jansen was suddenly on the ground with his cane kicked away, holding up his hands to fend off Simeon who stood over him.

Chapter Five

"Simeon, stop!" Jonathan cried, holding back his friend from beating up the old man.

"He's a traitor!" Simeon hissed.

"Leave him be!"

Simeon's face registered disbelief. "You're taking his side?"

"I'm on your side."

"If that were true, you wouldn't be defending him."

"I'm defending his freedom, same as I would yours."

Simeon shook his head. "If you are defending a Tory, then you are defending the king." He kept shaking his head as if he couldn't believe what he was hearing.

Jonathan had never seen his friend so angry. The humor had completely drained from his face and his abundant energy had lost its boyish charm, instead it now seemed ominous.

"Move away from him, Simeon. He's just an old man," Jonathan said.

Simeon raised his fist as Mr. Jansen cowered, holding up his hands in front of his face.

"Simeon!" Mrs. Stone said sharply. "Drop your fists."

"You've always been on the fence, Mrs. Stone. Now I know your true feelings. You're a traitor, just like the old man."

It was Jonathan who threw the first punch. His fist landed on Simeon's cheek and there was an audible crunch. He pulled his hand back, the pain blistering. Yet he brought his arm back for another go.

"No, Jonathan!" Mrs. Stone cried.

With what space he had in the crowd, Simeon charged Jonathan and knocked him over. They landed on the ground in a tangle of limbs and both rose quickly, ready again to strike.

People around them seemed torn between berating the boys for fighting and trying to ignore them in order to pay attention to Colonel Crafts.

Colonel Crafts carried on, his booming voice rising and falling as he listed the shortcomings of the King's offenses, evidence of his tyranny over the colonies, and thus justification for the colonies' revolt.

Seeing more punches about to be thrown, Mrs. Stone stepped between Jonathan and Simeon. "Boys, stop! You are not each other's enemy. Are you listening? Are you hearing what true injustice sounds like? Listen to the Colonel, I beg you!"

"Hush, all of you," said a woman standing nearby. "I want to hear what else the king is guilty of."

"Can't you take your fight somewhere else?" said a young woman wearing spectacles.

A young man in a smart-looking suit said, "Please consider removing yourselves from this square. I have no desire to miss this moment in history on account of a disagreement between two hot-blooded boys." A child held the young man's hand and glared at Jonathan.

Impossibly, Colonel Crafts' voice grew even louder and he seemed to be speaking now directly to Jonathan and Simeon.

Simeon turned toward his employer and slowly, slowly, unclenched his fists. He kept shaking his head, and after taking one last look at Jonathan, he moved sideways into the crowd, which folded in around him until he disappeared altogether.

Mr. Jansen was hurt, that was very clear. He lay on the ground, groaning, trying to reach for his cane.

"Help him," Mrs. Stone ordered.

"Yes, Mother."

With considerable effort, they helped Mr. Jansen to his feet, He stood awkwardly, rubbing his elbows, bewildered by the fall.

Jonathan found his cane and returned it to him. He clutched it, his knuckles white.

"I love my country," he mumbled. "God

save the king." He seemed to be having difficulty breathing. Jonathan thought of the medicine he had not taken.

"Are you okay?" said Jonathan.

Mr. Jansen rubbed his chest, his pain evident.

Mrs. Stone felt his pulse.

"I can't breathe so well," he said, his face pale.

As he said this, Colonel Crafts thundered, *"We, therefore, the Representatives of the United States of America, in General Congress, assembled, appealing to the supreme judge of the world for the rectitude of our intentions, do, in the name, and by authority of the good people of these colonies, solemnly publish and declare, that these United Colonies are, and of right ought to be free and independent states; that they are absolved from all allegiance to the British crown, and that all political connection between them and the state of Great Britain, is and ought to be totally dissolved."*

At "totally dissolved," the crowd lost all restraint and erupted into wild cheering and applause.

Colonel Crafts continued on to the end but the crowd had heard all they needed to hear. In particular, the words, "United States of America."

The words, the name, rang in Jonathan's ears. So that is how the colonies would be, after the war, after they won. They would be united. That was the answer he had needed. They would be the United States of America. He said the words out loud. "United States of America."

Supporting Mr. Jansen on her arm, Mrs. Stone heard Jonathan and smiled. "It sounds good."

"It sure does."

Mr. Jansen scoffed. "United, bah. Easier said than done. You watch. It won't go as you all dream it will. Your experiment will fail. You'll need the king to come back in and fix your problems. You watch and see."

"Are you admitting we stand a chance of winning this war, Mr. Jansen?"

If Jonathan had thought Mr. Jansen was warming to him, after all they had been through today, he was wrong.

Mr. Jansen growled. "The king will win! The king will win! You will all hang for treason before the year is done. That is how your little rebellion will go. King George will never let the colonies go."

"You are stuck in Boston, without soldiers to protect you, without King George's support. Why aren't you afraid?"

Mr. Jansen narrowed his eyes. "I am an old man, dead at any minute. What do I have to be afraid of? What can be done to me? Some pain, maybe? I have felt more pain than you can possibly know."

"My father is dead. That is pain enough."

Mr. Jansen studied him for a moment. "Ay, lad. That is pain enough," he said.

The afternoon heat had intensified, as had people's emotions in reaction to hearing

Colonel Crafts' reading of the Declaration of Independence.

Mr. Jansen continued shouting, "Long live the king!" as loudly as his failing voice would allow.

More than one person looked at him with such acrimony that Jonathan began to fear for the man's safety.

"The crowd is restless," Jonathan said.

"Yes," Mrs. Stone said. "I don't like it."

Their attention was drawn to the House, where men had climbed onto to the roof through the window and were sawing off the unicorn and lion.

From below, the crowd cheered them on.

The statues stood taller than the men themselves and proved cumbersome to dismantle, but more men emerged from the window and joined the effort and soon enough the lion and unicorn were being lowered by rope down to the street where throngs of people accepted them and carried them into the center of the square, heaving them awkwardly to rest against each other. The lion lay on its side, its mouth open in something like a roar, something like a smile. The unicorn lay against the lion, its horn pointing to the harbor, its tongue protruding from its wooden mouth.

Although the lion and unicorn represented the monarchy and King George's tyranny over the colonies, they were beautiful carvings and must have taken a craftsman many, many hours of work to create. Seeing them treated so carelessly didn't seem right.

The sight of the lion and the unicorn treated thus seemed to have an effect on Mr. Jansen that perhaps Simeon would have liked to witness. His bravado suddenly shrank. He now stood rather small, his shoulders hunched and his chin lowered. He clutched Jonathan's arm. "What will be done with them?" he whispered hoarsely.

"I don't know, Mr. Jansen."

"Those beautiful carvings."

Soon enough, his question was answered.

People brought logs of wood and set them beneath the statues. Papers of all kinds were crumpled up and thrown into the mix.

Other items bearing emblems of royalty were hauled out of buildings, thrown from windows, and added to the pile, including the king's arms from the Court House.

"No," Mr. Jansen gasped.

And then came Simeon, holding a blazing torch, his mouth set firmly. His face was void of its usual mirth. He walked around the life-size carved animals, setting fire to the paper and logs beneath.

In the heat of the day, with the sun beating down, the lion and unicorn began to burn.

People seemed hardly to breathe until the flames took hold and the blaze grew in size and heat, and then cheering burst forth and the crowd lost all inhibition and set to celebrating, although Jonathan heard, too, shouts of disapproval.

"We need to leave. Now," said Mrs. Stone. But instead of moving away from the bonfire, the crowd pressed in and moved them closer. They were caught in the flow of people and no amount of pushing could shift their course.

Chapter Six

Mr. Jansen was now holding onto Jonathan for dear life. His eyes were large with fear. Jonathan and his mother linked arms so they wouldn't be separated. They drew closer to the fire, and still closer. The heat coming off the burning statues intensified and sweat poured down their faces.

"Just don't get separated," said Mrs. Stone, stumbling over someone's feet and nearly falling.

Jonathan felt himself protector of both his mother and Mr. Jansen. He fought his own fear, worrying first for their safety, and drew himself to his full height, expanding his shoulders to their full breadth, wanting to cry out for his father, wanting to be small again so that he didn't need to sort through the questions of freedom, of violence, of death, of all the worries and fears that seemed to expand in number and intensity the older he got.

There had been a time when his father would sit on the porch in the evening, Jonathan beside him, and they would watch whatever was before them, a bird, maybe, or the trees bowing and shaking in the wind, or the sun setting behind the hills. They shared that quiet hour of the day, savoring it like two people sharing a slice of pie. Sometimes Mother would join them. She was always welcome, but mostly she read during that hour, happy for her own quiet. She must have known, too, Jonathan thought, how a father and son sometimes needed to be just father and son.

Jonathan hadn't experienced that kind of quiet in a long time now. He suddenly missed his father so much his heart felt like it might break all over again. If he were here, he would explain things to Jonathan, tell him how freedom is messy sometimes, how freedom doesn't mean perfection but a country's willingness to face what is wrong and try to fix it for the betterment of all people.

All people.

He looked at Mr. Jansen.

If Jonathan believed in freedom for all people, if he believed in the liberty of the United States of America as described by Colonel Crafts, then he had an obligation to live out that belief even if he didn't want to. Even if, to someone like Simeon, his actions might seem untrue to the cause.

They were close to the bonfire now, which was brilliant even in the bright afternoon sun. The heat was intense. The unicorn and lion were slow to burn but had noticeably lost their shape, their heroic postures. It seemed a waste, burning those beautiful sculptures. And yet he knew the fire was a symbolic severing of ties with England, a symbolic forging of a new country.

The faces of those around him reflected mixed emotions. Some seemed to be thinking of loved ones already killed, some held their children and perhaps wondered how many loved ones they were still to lose. Still others stood quietly in reflection, perhaps seeing this moment as an explanation for the violence they had been victims of, or perhaps justification for violence they had done.

And then there were those who were jubilant. On the other side of the fire Jonathan could see Simeon's red hair among those who danced, among those who understood the war in simple terms, who believed King George was to blame for every injustice, every hungry child, every death.

Jonathan blamed King George, too, but he also remembered his father saying, "No one in war is blameless. Not even I."

The biggest feeling around the fire, however, was one of unity. They knew now what they were fighting for. Independence had been declared. Officially. Were they independent now? Or would they be independent after the war? Jonathan supposed it didn't matter.

One single document, that's all that had been read. One single piece of paper, written by men as flawed as anyone, and the people of Boston's will to fight had been reenergized.

The same would be true for all the cities in which the Declaration of Independence had been read. Many cities, many people, all of the colonies would be given words to name their fears and dreams and feel a sense of unity desperately needed in the continued fight against England.

The three of them stood watching the flames, pressed in on all sides, listening to the cheering crowd.

Jonathan felt like a spectator. The party seemed premature. They hadn't won the war yet. And maybe they wouldn't win the war. What was certain was that many, many more lives would be lost. And yet, he knew, they celebrated not because victory had been declared but because the independence had been declared. Independence had been declared! The war had a purpose. It had a name. The colonies had a name. The United States of America.

The lion's crown had burned all the way down, the unicorn's horn also. As their faces caved in to the flames, Mr. Jansen began to cry, tears streaming down his face.

Mrs. Stone's face was grim, the grief lines around her mouth deeply etched.

And in that moment Jonathan made up his mind. "Follow me, Mother," he said. "Hold on tight to Mr. Jansen."

"I have him," she replied.

Jonathan took a deep breath. "Okay, here we go." He lowered one shoulder, lowered his head, and slowly, firmly, began pushing his way through the crowd.

At first no one budged.

Jonathan pressed on.

"Wrong way, friend," someone grumbled.

"Didn't expect to see you out here, Jansen," someone else said. "Does the king know you're here? Sorry showing for the likes of you."

Still someone else said, "That boy's got the right idea. I don't trust this crowd."

No one moved aside for them willingly, but Jonathan was undeterred. He pushed and pushed, not forcefully, but firmly, apologizing as they went along.

After a great deal of effort and a great many apologies, the spaces between people gradually widened and finally they were free.

Catching their breath, they sought relief from the heat under the awning of a one-story brick building.

No one said anything. They were lost in thought, as sometimes happens, Jonathan had been learning, when momentous things happen in life and people need time to make sense of what they had just seen or experienced.

Though tired-looking, his mother did not seem otherwise hurt or fatigued. He had seen her safely out of the crowd. His father would have been proud.

Mr. Jansen, however, did not appear well. His breathing was laborious and he bent over in obvious pain. The dried tears on his dirt-streaked face compounded his run-down air. Suddenly, he crumpled to the ground.

"Mr. Jansen!" Mrs. Stone cried, rushing to him and seeking to bring him some relief by loosening his tie. "Water, please!" she called to those walking past. No one paid her any mind.

"Jonathan," she said, "Run back to Mr. Jansen's home. Fetch his medicine and bring it here. Quick now!"

"Yes, Mother." Jonathan ran down State Street and turned the corner at the hat shop owned by Mr. Weston. The shop was closed now. Jonathan remembered seeing Mr. Weston at the reading. Everyone must have been at the reading.

Shops all along the way looked hastily locked, all business temporarily abandoned.

Two more blocks and he arrived at Mr. Jansen's home. Mr. Jansen had forgotten to lock the front door and so Jonathan thrust it open and ran straight to the hallway desk. He grabbed the small bottle of pills and was about to run back when he caught sight of the painting hanging above the desk. It wasn't a large painting, but something about the colors made him pause to have a quick second look.

The scene depicted a red-haired queen riding on horseback through throngs of adoring people. The old-fashioned clothing worn by the people in the painting indicated the queen to be Queen Elizabeth, the last Tudor monarch. She was a woman his mother admired very much.

"She kept England in peace for forty-four years," his mother marveled. "No king was ever as brave or as clever as she."

So, Mr. Jansen also admired Queen Elizabeth. This little piece of common ground made Jonathan think more kindly toward the old man. It was also a reminder of the cultural heritage his mother was denying by supporting the revolution. Her struggle could not have been easy.

Jonathan pocketed the medicine, fetched a glass of water from the pitcher on the washstand, and as carefully and quickly as possible, retraced his steps back to the State House.

CHAPTER SEVEN

When Jonathan arrived, Mr. Jansen was sitting on a chair someone had produced, with his head resting against the brick wall.

Judge Mariner stood at his side, listening intently as Jonathan's mother spoke. They both studied Mr. Jansen with concern.

Mrs. Stone looked up as Jonathan approached. "Oh, good, Jonathan, you're here." She held out her hand and he dug in his pocket for the pills. As his mother managed the pill bottle, he knelt by Mr. Jansen and coaxed him into taking a small bit of water.

Judge Mariner presided over their efforts to revive Mr. Jansen. "Your friend will be all right, I think," he said.

Jonathan was about to correct him, to tell him Mr. Jansen was not their friend, only their customer, but then he thought better of it and simply nodded.

His mother gave him a meaningful look. To Judge Mariner, she said, "He will be all right. The medicine will help. The water will help, too."

"I often find your ginger tea to be a great asset in reviving my own spirits, Mrs. Stone."

"Indeed, ginger works wonders for ailments of many kinds. And we will make sure Mr. Jansen drinks a little of it when we see him safely home."

But at least five minutes passed before Mr. Jansen revived, and even then he was visibly weakened.

"He will need assistance in returning home," Judge Mariner said.

"I think you're right," Mrs. Stone replied.

"Will you accept my offer of sending for my carriage?"

Mrs. Stone hesitated, but she could see the practicality of the offer and could not refuse, considering Mr. Jansen's condition. "Your offer is very kind. I accept—we accept."

"Wonderful. I will be back shortly."

Mrs. Stone tended to Mr. Jansen. "Take more water, you badly need cooling down."

Mr. Jansen did not argue. Jonathan wondered if his spirit now suffered more than his body. The fight seemed to have gone out of him.

Mr. Jansen wiped his mouth. His head hung low.

"You will soon feel better," Mrs. Stone told him. "A proper cup of tea, a bit of rest, and you will feel like yourself again, you will see." She fanned him with her bonnet.

"You are very kind," he said hoarsely.

"We may be divided on politics, but we are still neighbors, are we not?"

Mr. Jansen cleared his throat. Tears sprang to his eyes. "A little more water, please."

Mrs. Stone helped him take another drink.

"Thank you," he said.

"Judge Mariner is bringing his coach."

"I live only three blocks from here."

"Nevertheless." She continued fanning

him with her bonnet and he seemed to accept that for the moment he could not argue with her. He closed his eyes.

Jonathan observed his mother. Her hair was in disarray and her cheeks were flushed from the heat of the day and its adventures, and he thought there was a liveliness in her eyes he had not seen in a long time, a kind of sureness to her movements. The lines of grief were still there, but they appeared less heavy, less burdensome.

How could this change have happened so quickly, he wondered. Was it because she finally decided where she stood on the war? A warring mind is a terrible thing, he knew.

"Jonathan," Mrs. Stone said.

Jonathan looked to where she was pointing.

Simeon walked on the other side of the road, flanked by two other boys, their arms around each other. They were laughing and whooping. Simeon's face was flushed, his hair grimy from the smoke, his clothes rumpled. When he saw Jonathan, he didn't stop, he didn't acknowledge him. His eyes moved from Jonathan to Mrs. Stone to Mr. Jansen. He patted the other boys' shoulders and the one wearing a lopsided hat hollered, "Death to traitors!"

The boys laughed and Simeon cast Jonathan a look over his shoulder as they carried on down the street. Jonathan couldn't decipher the look's meaning, but he didn't feel he needed to. His friend was no longer his friend. That much was clear. Jonathan had lost a friend and gained—he looked at Mr. Jansen—what, exactly?

Maybe it wasn't about Mr. Jansen. Maybe, what he had gained was an understanding of this new country and its experiment with freedom. He had so much to learn.

Judge Mariner returned with his carriage. He hopped out nimbly and helped Mr. Jansen stand.

Mrs. Stone held open the door to the carriage while Judge Mariner and Jonathan assisted

Mr. Jansen. His breathing had not yet evened out and every step seemed painful.

The ride to his house lasted all of two minutes, but had they walked, Jonathan doubted whether the old man would have made it without needing to be carried.

"You're very kind to have allowed the use of your carriage, sir," Jonathan said to Judge Mariner as they exited the carriage.

"It is nothing."

"Kindness is not nothing. Kindness requires courage. Today, I understand the truth of that more than ever."

Judge Mariner nodded thoughtfully. "Those are wise words from someone so young."

"I'm not so young."

"No. I misspoke. I apologize. Wise words, nonetheless. Your mother must be very proud of you."

Jonathan glanced at his mother helping Mr. Jansen settle into a chair by the window. "I don't know. One day, I hope."

"You are well on your way, I expect." Judge Mariner smiled. "Well," he continued, "I must return to my daughter." He tipped his hat. "Mrs. Stone. Jonathan."

Mrs. Stone rose and escorted the judge to the door. "Give my regards to your daughter," she said.

"Sarah will be most pleased."

"Thank you again for your help. It came at a time when it seemed we had no friends in the world."

"Helping one's neighbor is an obligation and a privilege, I know you will agree. I hope to see you again soon, Mrs. Stone."

Mrs. Stone inclined her head, neither affirming nor denying his hope.

"Good day."

"Good day, to you."

After Judge Mariner left, Jonathan realized how good it had felt to have the judge in charge of things, however briefly. Now that he was gone, Jonathan again felt the weight of responsibility.

"How is he?" he said to his mother, who had turned her attention to preparing a kettle for tea.

"He doesn't look well," Mrs. Stone said softly. "A little tea might help, and a good deal of rest, but I believe something inside of him was hurt when Simeon threw him down, a bruised or cracked rib, perhaps."

"Should I fetch the doctor?"

"Mr. Jansen says he does not wish to see one. He says all the king-honoring doctors have left and he refuses to be seen by one of us Patriots."

Jonathan was unhappy to hear his mother's view on Mr. Jansen's health, but when she said, "one of us Patriots," he smiled in spite of himself.

Evidently, she knew what he was smiling about. "Yes, Jonathan. Smile away. I'm no longer on the fence, you see?"

They had more to talk about but Mrs. Stone wanted to make sure Mr. Jansen had everything he needed before they left. She asked Jonathan to help him to bed while she made something for him to eat for dinner.

It took considerable effort to help the man to his bedroom. Mr. Jansen sat down heavily on the bed while Jonathan removed his shoes and drew down the covers.

"I hurt all over," Mr. Jansen said. "Every bone, every muscle. I am tired." He lay down. Jonathan helped him lift his feet into the bed. "Maybe I won't wake up. That would be okay, I think."

"You are going to wake up," said Jonathan, "Or, if you are not awake when my mother and I check on you in the morning, we will wake you up. With a bucket of cold water, if need be."

"You wouldn't dare. I'll tell the king on you."

Jonathan laughed. "I would expect nothing less, although from what I can tell, the king has other more pressing matters to tend to."

Mrs. Stone came into the room and set a

plate of buttered bread, cheese, and another cup of tea on the table beside the bed. "If you wake and are hungry, Mr. Jansen, here is a plate for you."

Hardly moving his hand, he motioned them toward the door. "Go away," he said. "Give an old man a little peace."

"We will check on you in the morning," Mrs. Stone said, following Jonathan to the door.

Already Mr. Jansen was snoring.

"Will he be okay?" said Jonathan.

"His spirits are returning, at least." She sighed. "I think he will be fine, but his recovery will be slow. We'll know more tomorrow. A good rest is what he really needs."

They spent some time tidying up the house, making sure the water pitcher was full, the hallway swept, the wood box full in case there should be a change in temperature and a fire necessary.

As they moved about, Jonathan saw his mother pause, looking at the painting of

Queen Elizabeth. He couldn't decipher the emotions on her face, nor did he feel the need to. They were for her alone.

When Mrs. Stone felt the house was in good order, they checked on Mr. Jansen once more, drew his blanket up to protect him from the night air, and began to make their way home.

It was evening now. The sun was going down slowly behind the rooftops, leaving its golden glow reflecting in the windows and streets of the city.

Even from blocks away, the sounds of the bonfire carried on, the smoke from it billowing like black snakes into the sky.

They walked in silence most of the way, sidestepping revelers and carriages.

When they neared their house, Mrs. Stone said, "So what's next, my son?"

"What do you mean?"

She stopped, so he did too. She faced him. "What's next in our fight for freedom?"

"I don't know, Mother."

"You are fourteen. The war will not end soon."

"Are you asking if I will fight one day?"

"You will soon be old enough."

Jonathan had considered this. He nodded slowly. "I feel it is my duty already. In two years I will feel even more that it is my duty. Father would not want us to let others earn our freedom for us."

Mrs. Stone didn't answer right away. They walked a little ways on, their steps unhurried. It seemed like the first time today they had time to move slowly, to enjoy each other's company.

They greeted neighbors, customers, their friends.

"The city suddenly feels more like my own," Mrs. Stone said.

"It's a brave town."

"It is a brave country." Mrs. Stone stopped and turned to Jonathan. "Before you leave to fight, you will go to school again, you will study, and you will help me make our business steadfast."

"All right, Mother."

"What other fruit can we turn into tea?"

Jonathan had ideas about that. "Other berries, very likely. Blueberries, blackberries, even cranberries. We'll try all different sorts." He linked his arm to hers. "And what did you make of the words of the Declaration of Independence? Did John Adams do a fine job?"

"I believe Thomas Jefferson is to be given most of the credit, but yes, it was mighty fine writing, don't you agree?"

"It was. The words were very moving. I would like to write like that one day."

Mrs. Stone squeezed his arm. "You have it in you. With practice."

Jonathan felt more grownup this evening than he did this morning. Can growing up happen so fast like that? In just one day?

"The United States of America," Mrs. Stone said. "How about that."

"The United States of America," Jonathan

said, breathing in the evening air. "Let's see what we can do."

The American Revolution

The American Revolution took place between 1775 and 1783. It was a period in which the Patriots of the thirteen American colonies fought against the Loyalists of England for their freedom.

The colonies fought for freedom, but didn't know exactly what their freedom would look like once won. The process of becoming a nation was slow and painful. Representatives from the thirteen colonies met in Philadelphia. They became known as the Continental Congress and together they wrote many documents that gave shape to the revolution.

The Declaration of Independence was one such document. It was first read in Philadelphia on July 4, 1776, and then read in other cities throughout the colonies, including Boston on July 18. For the first time, Patriots heard the name "United States of America," and the words served to galvanize the colonists into war against King George. Thomas Jefferson was the main author of the Declaration of Independence. Benjamin Franklin, John Adams, Roger Sherman, and Robert Livingston formed the rest of the committee that determined the focus of the pamphlet and assisted with revision.

George Washington was the Commander-in-Chief of the Continental Army during the war and was greatly respected and admired for his leadership. After the war, he became the first President of the United States.

Q & A
with Sam George

1. Why did you decide to write about the American Revolution?

It is a historical time period I wanted to know more about. Research is fun when you're interested in the topic, so I chose this period because I knew the work involved would be a pleasure.

2. What is one thing you were fascinated by?

Just one? I loved reading the entire Declaration of Independence. It's a powerful document.

3. Who is one historical figure you were impressed by?

George Washington, of course! Also, Abigail Adams.

About the Author

Sam George is the author of many books for young people. He lives with his family in California and spends a lot of time watching hummingbirds zing around his yard.

Websites to Visit

www.boston1775.blogspot.com

www.boston-tea-party.org

www.theamericanrevolution.org

Writing Prompt

As you get older, you gain more responsibility. When you take those responsibilities seriously, you may gain more freedom and flexibility at home and school. Write your own Declaration of Independence that highlights the freedoms you want to have as a maturing young person, and support those declarations with examples that show why those freedoms should be granted to you. Consider the reasons your parents and/or teachers may oppose granting those freedoms, and respectfully counter those arguments within your document.